THE PINNACLE

THE MAKER'S PLAN

ADIL RASOOL KHAWAJA

ISBN 979-888555104-5

My dedication came from my love for writing. I was always a writer and when i heard of notion press, i become super excited, because this platform gave me the kick I needed.

Contents

Preface

The Pinnacle is a book which links my imagination with my fantasies. I wrote this book because I loved watching anime and secondly people in my country mostly stay away from writing books that involves Gods and his disciples. They generally think that this is a very bad thing to do and think that this activity, in some way, shape or form goes against religion. I am a very imaginative person, I love to imagine things and the idea of the book really piqued my interest, hence I would recommend everyone to right what you imagine and take pride in doing so.

Now I really adored anime like Dragon Ball Z, The Misfit of Demon King Academy, High School DXD and Noragami. These anime were about how the Gods and The Demons fought each other for power. The supernatural and sci-fi genera really intrigued me. Intrigued me to the point of me becoming an otaku. My motivation came from having an interest in these types of genera, as they really piqued my interest. So, when our instructor told us that we would be writing a book, on whatever topic we could think off, I got excited. So before attempting to write this book, I watched these shows repeatedly, I did this to understand the plot better and to understand how I can duplicate the plot of these animes make into my book.

1 The Old War

Once upon a time, both Satan and the seven princes of hell joined forces with each other and assembled a huge army to overthrow God. They succeed in destroying most of the creations of God, but God was so strong that he stopped them in their tracks. God, knowing that even with their combined strength it still won't be enough to inflect the smallest of damage to him, gave them a chance and told them to seek forgiveness and atone for their sins against all the creations they destroyed. Satan and the seven princes of hell were hesitant to accept defeat and charged on. God seeing this banished them to hell and sealed them there. God then held a conference with his angels, the conference was held to discuss the fate of Satan, the seven princes and all of hell. The angels suggested total annihilation, but God had other plans. God gave out the commandment that he wouldn't destroy them, but he will form such a being that would lead to their destruction. A messenger angel was sent by God to hell to inform the inhabitants of hell about the commandment.

(The commandment spread far and wide)

Satan (Amazed): Well well well, so God isn't going to destroy us after all.

Mammon: But my Lord, God did say he was going to form a being which would lead to our destruction.

Satan (Anger): Do you really think, God can create a creation which would rival our strength.

Leviathan: FIRE, is strong. FIRE ECLIPSES ALL.

Satan: Yes Leviathan, we are the pinnacle of strength and together no being in the whole cosmos can overcome our demonic powers.

Beelzebub: AHHAHAHAHHAHA, ALL HAIL SATAN!

Asmodeus: HAIL SATAN!

Belphegor: HAIL SATAN!

Satan: Now we must wait for the creation of this so called powerful being.

17 years Pass and a huge crowd of millions of angels are seen around God's Castle in heaven, anxiously waiting for His decision against the forces of hell.

God: My dear creation, witness my greatest creation, the creation that is above all previous creations and the creation that would lead to the destruction of all of hell.

On hearing this the angels all rejoice and send their praise to God.

God: A creation, which is simple, humane, strong, and most importantly made from my own blood.

God: I name thee "Adamazious".

(Angels quite down in disbelief)

Michael: All mighty, this is but a human.

God: Yes, that it is.

Michael: Humans cause war, bloodshed, slavery, and many other heinous things. Wouldn't an angel with all such qualities suffice?

God: Don't! contradict my decision, the one who stands before you is the pinnacle of power, strength, wisdom and above all else WRAITH.

Michael: Forgive me my Lord, for truly I am mistaken.

God: Don't ever give yourself to pride, it's what distinguishes you from the inhabitants of hell.
Michael: Your grace! Please forgive me as my judgement is flawed.
God: Worry not my servant, you are forgiven.
Michael: All HAIL GOD AND THE BIRTH OF ADAMAZIOUS
Gabriel: HAIL GOD! LONG LIVE ADAMAZIOUS!
Uriel: HAIL GOD! LONG LIVE ADAMAZIOUS!
Raphael: HAIL GOD! LONG LIVE ADAMAZIOUS!
Joel: HAIL GOD! LONG LIVE ADAMAZIOUS!

2

The News

The birth of Adamazious spread far across heaven and hell. Every known being sends their praise and rejoices the coming of great being which would end sorrow and bring about happiness and wisdom on to all dimensions and worlds.

Satan can be seen in hell, talking to Beelzebub about this creation and isn't fazed one bit.

Satan (Laughing): So, this is the so-called champion that God has made for our annihilation. Worthless waste of proper clay, what does God think? Does he really feel such a big can trample our great demonic being?

Beelzebub: My lord, the spiritual energy and raw mana around that creature is so intense. For a creature with so much power in its dormant state, do you think we can handle it when it reaches maturity?

Satan: These so-called creations of God are but weak. Even with the divine protection and divine blood inside of him, he is but a mere human at the end of the day.

Beelzebub: You are indeed the most magnificent and knowledge, Sire!

Satan: All we need to care about is to know where God is going to let this creature thrive.

Beelzebub: My lord! You need not worry but such problems. I, your servant, will keep a close eye on the information about this creature.

Satan: That is all!

Beelzebub: Sire!

After four hundred forty-five years pass, God makes a huge commandment about his new creation. All the creatures, big and small, come near the palace of God and eagerly wait for his announcement.

God: My dear creation, I have decided that now is the perfect time to send this creation of mine to the mortal world. But for my creations' sake, I have put a limit on his powers. I have done this so that he doesn't harm anyone nor anything. Adamazious will hence forth be sent down on Earth.

All the angels and other beings in heaven rejoice by cheering both their creator and his creation. This news spread like wildfire everywhere and to all beings, wherever they were. When this news reached the inhabitants of hell, they all started talking about it and the word reached to Satan's Palace.

Satan: So, God has chosen Earth. As expected, he would ultimately choose a planet which would inhabit by those insects(humans).

Mammon: What is your next command, Sire! Should we kill the child upon his birth?

Satan: No, the divine protection God has casted on him would be the strongest in the child's infancy state.

Mammon: What should we do then, Sire?

Satan: Wait while he is still a child and when he reaches adolescence and then we will prepare his execution. Until that happens, we can't do anything because the divine protection is too powerful for us to destroy.

Mammon: As you wish, Sire!

On Monday, 14th of June 29010, Adamazious was borned. He was brought up by the Truesdale family in the small village of Hogsfeet. The parents weren't wealthy and worked for very less pay. On the birth of Adamazious, light showers, accompanied by a rainbow, were seen by the parents. The parents knew that this wasn't no ordinary child, but a blessing sent by God himself. David and Ayesha named Adamazious "Theodore", which meant "gift from God".

They took immense care of the Theodore and didn't let him leave their sights.

As Theodore grew, people around started noticing the environment around themselves change. They thought he was a demon child at first but then after observing him, they thought that he had a good heart and demons don't generally have good hearts, so they really did believe that he was a gift from God. Unbelievable things started occurring, the environment, which was once barren, would become fertile and grew crops quicker than any other place in the world. His looks were so breath-taking that it was rumored that if you see his face, good things will happen to you. From early childhood, he was loved and respected by all around him. The village considered him a huge blessing from God and protected him from the evil which had enveloped the world.

When Theodore was six, he started to show extra-ordinary abilities. Theodore could easily speak four hundred different languages, he could lift seriously heavy object with ease, he could solve complex problems. He could talk with animals, he could sense harm even before it could take place, his reflexes were far better than any human, he could talk to the dead. But all these abilities happened on their own, Theodore wasn't aware of the abilities he possessed, because he was a child.

Theodore was a cheerful and wise human-being. He would never get into fights and would stay away from whatever he would consider wrong. This was mainly since God made him this way and since his parents taught him to be kind to everyone and stay away from causing or getting into trouble.

3

Tragedy

It was Theodore's birthday and to celebrate, he and his parents were going to the nearby market, this is the day when they came across the Wuhu gang. This gang was notorious for raping woman and murdering innocent people. Sickle, the gang's leader, touched Ayesha on her shoulder and pulled her back. Noticing this David rushed to protect his wife, but sickle got out a knife and made a huge puncture wound on David's arm. David was bleeding severely, and Theodore was crying because he didn't know what to do.

Ayesha: Stop David, just protect our child! He can't see this, leave me be and take him far away from here. Please!

David (On the ground, bleeding): I can't, if I leave you here, they will rape and murder you.

Ayesha: If this is the way my future is written, then let it happen. Protect my child at all costs. GO NOW!

Sickle: Awwwww, isn't that precious, the whore is worried about her family. David, I know you, always acting like you are so blessed by God. Let see what your God can do!

Sickle breaks Ayesha's neck Infront of David and Theodore. David goes silent and slowly reaches for his wife. He sees her twitching and cries; Theodore comes running to David and asks him why his mother is lying on the ground and not saying anything.

David (In full denial and with a low-pitched voice): Be...Because...Because she's DEAD!!!!!!!!!!!!!

Theodore (Constantly shaking David's shoulder): Dead? Will we see her again? Will she make food for us? Will she ever talk to us? Why aren't you answering me?

David (In disbelief): Her being dead makes you never see her again.

Theodore (Shaking): Wha..... Thi....... This can...... can't be happening.

Theodore starts to shake violently, the ground begins to shake, dark cloud covers the sky and furious winds begin to blow in the area. Theodore's hair starts to change color and his appearance starts to change as well. David sees this and starts to run towards Theodore.

David (Worried): Theodore what's happening to you?

Theodore (Angered): Sick......Sickl......SICKLE!!

Sickle: Bahahaha, so the whore's kid is a mana user? Huh, ok you sniveling son of a bitch, let's have ourselves a duel.

Sickle begins to power up, the ground starts to shake again and the gang members all retreat.

Theodore (Angered): Dad, leave this filth to me, take mom, and get her body away from this place.

David (Worried): I can't lose you too, your mother and I loved you to bits. I can't lose the both of you at the same time. Please stop this!!!!!!!!!!!!!!!!

Theodore: Father, I am serious, he is going to kill you regardless of the outcome of this duel, I don't want him to kill you. Please do what I say and leave with mom's body.

David understands and picks up Ayesha's body and tries to flee.

Sickle: Huh, where do you think you're going shithead. I am not finished with you yet. Buurzghaash!!!!!

Theodore (Quickly comes in front of David): Yati!!!!!!!!!!!!!!!

Sickle (Amazed): What? How is this possible? That was point-blank range. A seven-year-old child shouldn't be able to do such a thing. Shit!!! I need to get the hell out of here.

Theodore (Angered): What sort of a man are you, hurting innocents. Begone filth. Mkali wa Inferno!!!!!!!!!!!!!!!!!!!!

Sickle is instantly obliterated, and the blast leaves a huge crator in the ground. David is shocked and falls to his knees.

David (In disbelief): Oh no!!!! Theodore!!!!!!!!!!!!!!

Theodore instant appears behind David and asks him, where his mother is?

David (While still on his knees): She has left us Theo; she has left us for good.

Theodore sees the dead body of Ayesha and falls to his knees.

Theodore (Crying): Sorry mama, I couldn't protect you, I didn't know what to do. Please forgive me mama and come back to us, we really need you.

David (Crying): It's not your fault, my dear boy. Things happen and its all-what God wills.

Theodore: She always used to say that God loved everyone. Can't we ask God to return her back to us?

David (Looking at Theodore with helpless eyes): It doesn't work like that, my dear boy. God, indeed, loves everyone, and your mother is in heaven with God. God will keep her happy until the end of times.

Theodore: Can't we go to that place too?

David: We all must go there someday but we need to do good to get there.

Theodore: Sickle killed mama, what would happen to him?

David (Angered): He would go to hell and reside there for all of eternity. It's the fate of all evil doers like him.

Theodore: But papa, I killed him, will I also go to hell?

David: It is for God to decide, as he judges you on your intentions and you only did that to protect everyone. Now let's go and bury your mother in the village's old cemetery.

Both David and Theodore come back to the village and most of the people get scared of them. The gang members had told lies about Theodore being a demon child and that he would destroy everyone once he reached adolescence. They didn't get properly welcomed and most of the village folk kept distance from them due to the fear they had.

David and Theodore buried Ayesha and David said that it was time for him and Theodore to go back home. On the way, Theodore stopped and asked David that he had left something behind and will join him in some time. Theodore went to the graveyard and saw Ayesha's spirit sitting on her own gravestone. Theodore was surprised to see her.

Theodore: WAIT!!!!!!!! MAMA!!!!!!!!, you are still alive?

Ayesha's Spirit: My child, I am but a spirit now.

Theodore: A spirit?

Ayesha's Spirit: It's what we all become when we pass away from this world. Anyway, I wanted to tell you something.

Theodore: What is it mama's spirit?

Ayesha's Spirit: My dear son, don't put the blame of my death on your hands. As you are a child and children are pure beings. Please take care of your father and never do something which would make him sad.

Theodore: I will but mama..........

Before Theodore could say anything more, Ayesha's spirit started vanishing like sand blown with the wind. Theodore started crying but he vowed to himself to never earn his father's displeasure and to protect the things he held dear. He then hurried back home to his father. When he reached home, he found his father on the mattress, treating his wound. Theodore rushed to his father and hugged him. David's arm was very badly injured, and he was losing blood quickly. Theodore saw this and ran out of his house to get help. People, who loved him kept distance and avoided him because they thought with all those abilities he had, he must be a demon child. Theodore went from person to person and house from house, but no one was willing to help him. The thought of his father in pain made him beg people again and again. A shopkeeper instructed him to go look in the market and find a doctor there. Theodore rushed to the market and started looking for the doctor, he found the hut where the doctor was stationed but couldn't find the doctor in there. He asked people around and no one helped him. A few hours later, the doctor came back and entered his hut. Theodore rushed in his hut and told him what happened and asked for his help.

Theodore: Please doctor, help my father, he is badly injured.

Doctor: You are that demon child, right?

Theodore: No sir, my father is hurt badly, please help him. I'll do whatever you want, please help him!

Doctor: Ok child, lead me to your house.

Both the doctor and Theodore rush to check on David. They both reach the house and enter a dark room with David lying flat on the floor. The doctor hurriedly checks on him and asks Theodore to stay outside for a while. Sometime passes by and Theodore starts to peek inside. The doctor is seen down on his knees with his eyes covered. David had passed away with all the blood loss but leaves a note on the floor. Theodore enters the room and talks to the doctor.

Theodore: Sir, what's wrong with papa, is he going to be fine?

Doctor: My boy, your father has left you a note, please read it for yourself.

Theodore takes the note and begins to read, while reading he starts to cry. The note read:

"My dear Theo while you are reading this know that I have passed away. Don't be ashamed of what you did, it was meant to happen. From the moment you were born, your mother and I knew you were special, not because you bought us good fortune but because your mother and I were described as infertile. Having a child was the best thing that ever happened to us, it makes me sad that we didn't spend a long time with each other, but the days we spent with you were the best happiest ones in our lives. I know God will reunite us in the hereafter, so I wish you all the best for the times ahead.

Good-Bye My Dear Theo......"

The doctor immediately hugs Theodore and tells him to calm down. It suddenly starts to rain heavily, even though there were no clouds in the sky. The doctor sees this and holds Theodore close to him. He tells him that he will be by his side forever and asks him to live with him from now on. The doctor knows that Theodore is a very special child and due to that note, he considers himself as his father and guardian. He took Theodore to his house and told him that it was his house now and he could do whatever he wanted in there. Theodore was in such denial that he didn't utter a word and only replied by shaking his head up and down. The doctor then left him in his house and went to David's house, he picked up David's corpse and took it outside. He dug a grave and then gently lowered him down into the grave. After shoveling the soil over the David's grave, he sat down on his knees and he made a promise.

Doctor: I hope you can hear me David. I wished you had lived longer but it's God's plan, right? Regarding your son, you don't need to worry about him, I promise on my life that nothing bad will ever happen to him, I will do my best to keep him happy and healthy, rest in peace.

4

A New Beginning

It had been 10 years since the incident, but the doctor kept Theodore very close to him. The doctor cherished Theodore, he kept a very close eye on Theodore's health, and he loved him like he loved his own children. The doctor was a widower and had only one child, a girl named Jennae, age 17. Jennae was a calm and composed human being and she loved Theodore. Jennae used to leave halve of her meals and gave them to Theodore, but Theodore ate very little of it and usually wouldn't come to the dinner table. One day, Jennae asked her father about Theodore's back story. After hearing Theodore's past, the poor girl fell to her knees and let out a loud cry.

Jennae: How can someone live after experiencing such fatalities?

Doctor: I don't know how to answer that right now. But hear this child, don't ever make him feel sad nor let him down. He has already suffered enough.

Jennae: I will papa, him and I are going to best of friends, and I will do whatever it takes to protect him.

Doctor: That's my baby girl. Now go to bed, you have school tomorrow.

Jennae: Ahh, I almost forgot about that. Wait daddy, why don't you enroll Theo to my Modrose, School Of Witchcraft too? There he can make many friends and that could help him reconnect to the world.

Doctor That sounds like a great idea!!! Ill enroll him immediately.

The doctor calls the Principal and asks him about the enrollment of Theodore Truesdale. The best thing about Modrose, School Of Witchcraft, was that it was a boarding school for magic users, which is situated outside the village and this would be very good for him, as people wouldn't be shocked by his powers and will gladly accept him as one of their own. The Principal tells the doctor that he can bring him to the Modrose, School Of Witchcraft tomorrow, and he can start his studies from then on. The doctor goes to Theodore's room and tells him about his enrolment in Modrose, School Of Witchcraft, a school which would accept him for who he is and to help him understand and perfect his magic, so no one gets hurt. Theodore gently smiles and accepts the offer by just nodding his head up and down. The doctor then exists his house and goes to the local

The next day, the doctor asks his daughter to wake Theodore up and get him ready for school. Jennae runs towards Theodores room and asks him to wake up and get ready for school. Theodore gets up and dresses up. An hour passes by and the bus arrives, Jennae excitedly runs down the stairs and hugs her father and then gets aboard the bus. Theodore sees the affection the father and daughter have for each other and starts to cry a little. The doctor sees this and immediately hugs him and says everything is going to be fine. He tells him that he isn't alone in the world and he is right here whenever he needs anything. Theodore listens to his talks and hugs him tightly and then gives off a smile and gets aboard the bus.

The Modrose, School Of Witchcraft is one of the best in the whole world and is well known to produce highly skilled mana users. Gandalf, Alexander III, Storm Bringer, Hellspawn and Colt Sapphire are a few examples of great mana users this institute has produced. The courses were taught by some of the best spellcasters and renowned magic users in the world. It offered the best learning and practical environment for young and skilled mana users. The admission process is very simple, a person was test for spell usage, spell memory, spell execution and a power scale were made to test the person's capabilities and only the candidates with the best skills and execution were selected.

Jennae was already a student there, so she was exempted to take the admission test, but Theodore wasn't. So, while in the bus, the bus conductor dropped off Jennae at the Modrose, School Of Witchcraft entry gate and drove off. The bus conductor along with Theodore and a few other candidates stopped at the admission test center, opposite to the school execution yard. Theodore and the kids got off the bus and walked in, they were greeted by the Head Counselor.

Head Counselor: Good Morning!!! My name is Sir Draco Sapphire, I am the son of the mighty Colt Sapphire. Candidates hope you all are doing fine, so today my students, you will be tested whether you really belong here or not.

Jamie Lucus: Hurry it up wise guy! I must be somewhere.

Draco Sapphire: My my, what an energetic young fellow!! Right then proceed to the testing center everyone and give it your all!!!!

Theodore, Lucus and the rest of the kids, enter the testing center and are surprised to see that its blank. The place was empty, it looked like it was void of everything, a room with no doors, no windows and there was nothing to be seen. Sir Draco entered the room along with some guards and Sir Draco casts a spell and makes testing dolls appear.

Draco Sapphire: Your first test is to use the spell GAASH DUUMP. Lucus, why don't you do the honors.

Jamie Lucus: Call me by my first name old man and take a good look you weaklings. GAASH DUMMP!!!

The whole doll burns and becomes nothing but dust in a matter of moments. The kids get scared and all run away except Theodore, who isn't fazed but keeps his head down.

Draco Sapphire: So, you aren't all talk, great work. I see most of your comrades have forfeited, that's common during the admission tests. You!!! Theodore was it?

Theodore: Yes sir, my name is Theodore.

Draco Sapphire: Come on boy we don't have all day!

Jamie Lucus: What's with these cowards, hurry up and attempt the task you are given, worthless weakling.

Theodore: ....

Theodore walks a up to the testing platform and gets ready, he holds his hand out and takes a deep breath. A crimson aura starts to gush out of him, and Sir Draco see this and stops him.

Draco Sapphire: Oh, I don't think you have come to right place my dear. Get out of the Modrose and never show your face here ever again.

Theodore: But why sir, I never got to cast the spell.

Draco Sapphire: Didn't you hear me boy? Get the fuck out of my sight before I kill you myself!!

Theodore: I have been through a lot of sir, why are you doing this. The doctor told me that it was my first day at Modrose and that got me somewhat excited. You see I am an orphan, and the doctor is the nearest to a father figure I have. It would be a shame for me if I don't get enrolled.

Draco Sapphire: Boy you are really getting on my nerves now, get the fuck out of here before I turn you into dust.

Jamie Lucus: Theodore, get the fuck out right this instant, the old man's mana is increasing at a very alarming rate.

Theodore: I am not going anywhere; I will not put to shame anyone I hold dear anymore. Sir Draco, do you want to fight, bring it on!!

Draco Sapphire: You little shit, are you mocking me!!!!! I will end you!!!!!!!!!

Sir Draco charges and casts GAASH DUMMP on Theodore. The whole room erupts, and smokes covers the whole room.

Sir Draco: Huh, guess he was all talk and no bark. Lucus, get your ass ready for the next test.

Jamie Lucus: What have you done, are you crazy or something?

Sir Draco: Do you want to end up like him?

Jamie Lucus: No sir!!!

Draco Sapphire: Good, now get the fuck out of my sight.

Theodore: Wow and here I thought Lucus was weak. That was nothing sir, I didn't feel a thing.

Draco Sapphire: How the FUCK DID YOU SURVIVE THAT, it was a point-blank attack, it should have killed you.

Theodore: Really? Is it my turn now?

Draco Sapphire: Huh, try your best shot, squirt!!!

Theodore starts to release his crimson aura again; the room starts to crumble. The winds start to blow wildly, the floor beneath them starts to shake and the whole room becomes crimson red.

Draco Sapphire: What is this pressure? What are you boy?

Theodore: I'm your reckoning!!! GAASH DUMMP!!!!!!!!!!!!!!!!!!!!!!!

Sir Draco narrowly escapes the explosion and attempts to run away while he has a chance. Theodore catches him.

Theodore: You said, "bring it on Squirt", are you scared of me? Does my power scare you? Do you think you can survive?

Draco Sapphire: You won't get away with this, BOY!

Jamie Lucus: Stop it now!!!!!!!! You monster!

Theodore: You think its all about you isn't it?

Theodore throws Sir Draco across the room and walks towards Jamie Lucus.

Jamie Lucus: No! please forgive me!!! I never meant it!!!

Theodore: Well.... I think that's enough of a performance for now!

Theodore faints and falls to the ground. Sir Draco and Jamie, start talking to one another about what just happened.

Jamie Lucus: What was that sir, is he what I think he is?

Draco Sapphire: I can't say anything for now boy but this young one is something else. You both pass the admission trail.

and congratulations.

Jamie Lucus: But sir what about the other tests? And why are you enrolling him? Isn't he too dangerous?

Draco Sapphire: I don't think you two need to be tested further, you guys are very powerful. The way I see it you aren't going to utter one word about this, but rest assured it looks like he has some control over his powers but if he goes energy ballistic, the headmaster will see him.

Sir Draco Sapphire picks up Theodore and asks Jamie to go into his dorm room and get ready for the induction ceremony. Sir Draco carries Theodore to the school's doctor and tells the doctor to take care of him and be careful at the sometime.

5

The Induction Ceremony

After the admission exam, Theodore finds himself on the school's nursing room. He sees the nurse and has a conversation with her about what had happened?

Theodore: Excuse me madam, how did I end up like this?

Nurse: I think you fainted because you used too much of your mana in that admission test.

Theodore: Oh, is everyone with me fine, I kind of lost it in there.

Nurse: They are more then fine, some bruises here and there but are very healthy.

Theodore: Sorry for that, I tend to over express sometimes, but I can't control it.

Nurse: Oh! You came to the right place, the induction ceremony is almost about to start and while you are there, go for the "Insignia Archetype".

Theodore: Will it help me?

Nurse: It will help you keep a firm control over your mana usage but a keep in mind it's a very low scale archetype. Students mostly use archetypes like Angelic, Light-Sworn, and War.

Theodore: Oh! I really like this archetype, thank you very much madam, I will always remember this favor!

Nurse: Bless your heart, young man! Now get up and attend the induction ceremony. Ask the janitor for help, he will take you to your room and when you get there put on your dress and join the ceremony.

Theodore: Will do!

Theodore rushes outside and asks the janitor to help him get to his room. The janitor takes Theodore to his private room and there Theodore gets dressed. After getting dressed, the janitor takes him to the auditorium where the ceremony would be held.

When entering the auditorium, he is shocked to see the number of people there. Jennae finds him and rushes to him.

Jennae: Hey! Theo where were you, the ceremony started 30 minutes ago.

Theodore: Sorry! I had problems putting these clothes on, hahaha.

Jennae: You look great Theo!

Theodore: You to Jennae, you look spectacular.

Jennae: Oh you! Hey, I want you to meet someone, she is a very good friend of mine.

Theodore: Oh! Who would that be?

Jennae takes Theodore to her friend, Malissa Armstrong.

Jennae: Hey! Malissa this was the guy I told you about!

Malissa Armstrong: Wait you mean this guy defeated the mighty Sickle?

Jennae: Yeah, my father said he was crazy strong!

Malissa Armstrong: I don't believe this, let me get out my mana reader right now, I don't think this guy has the strength to beat someone as mighty as Sickle.

Theodore: Well, its not that simple, I need to be angry first.

Malissa Armstrong: You are hopeless and here I was excited to meet someone very strong. What a buzzkill you turned out to be!

Jennae: Come on you two stops fighting, it's almost time for Theodore's archetype selection!

Malissa Armstrong: Wait let me guess, you are going to choose the "Insignia" Archetype, aren't you?

Theodore: Wow, how did you know that?

Malissa Armstrong: You serious? That's so lame, Thanks Jennae for wasting my time on a twerp. At least try to look good by faking to go into a stronger archetype. You disgust me!

Jennae: Malissa! That's very rude! Apologize to Theodore right now!

Theodore: I don't think there is any need to fight both of you.

Malissa Armstrong: Oh, shut it! I am out of here!

Jennae: Forget her Theo, don't know what's got into her.

Theodore: Its no problem, most of the people here are like that, they really value power over everything.

Jennae: So, you are going to pick Insignia Archetype, right? Do you know what the archetype provides you?

Theodore: Not exactly but the lovely nurse lady told me that I can have better control over my powers with it.

Jennae: Oh! That's so cool, well the seminar is going to start anyway, you can have a firm understanding of all the archetypes.

Theodore: Oh great, will you be joining?

Jennae: No Theodore, I already have an archetype, I with the light-sworn, also known as the medical school.

Theodore: Oh, so you are a healer then?

Jennae: Yes, and a good one at that. Look at the time! I am late for class, good luck Theo!

Jennae leaves Theodore to attend her class and Theodore walks into the seminar room. Everything is nearly complete, and the program looked like it would start at any moment. Theodore sees Sir Draco Sapphire enter the room and suddenly students start to gather into the room. The room was quickly filled with students, some repeaters, and some transfer students. Theodore finds Jamie Lucus and rushes to sit beside him. Lucus happily offers him a seat and they both sit together.

Draco Sapphire: Greeting Students, welcome to your induction ceremony, hope you really enjoyed each other's company and are excited for today's shortlisting.

Theodore: This is the archetype thing, right?

Jamie Lucus: Yes, Theodore.

Draco Sapphire: Each student will be admitted into an archetype today. So, it is important that I tell you about the archetypes first. So, let's start off with the WAR Archetype, students admitted into this archetype receive training of magic, categorized into three points. As it is a physical dominant archetype, when the first point is reached, also known as the Marauder, it will allow the user to gain 25% more power to his base strength, with added benefits like: Faster reflexes, higher durability, higher stamina, and resistance to mind-control. Reach the second point, also known as the Achilles, it will allow the user to gain 50% more power to his base strength and the benefits remain the same but the sharpness of each benefit increases. Lastly, when the third point is reached, also known as the Dark Corner, it will allow the user to gain 100% more power to his base strength and the benefits remain the same, but the sharpness of each benefit increases times five. One shouldn't go this far but if the situation is dire and this is your last option, only then use it. It is believed that if Dark Corner is achieved, the effect on the user's body can range from seriously disfigured to permanent paralysis. This is basically due to all the mana overflows in the body and if one isn't trained enough, it could be the end for them.

Theodore: This sounds so cool!

Jamie Lucus: So, are you going to pick the WAR archetype?

Theodore: No, I still need to hear out the rest to decide.

Draco Sapphire: Next comes the Light-Sworn Archetype, they generally described as the doctors of the mana world. Like the WAR archetype, they also receive training of magic and along with magic they are taught how to make healing potions. There are no points for this archetype, as this archetype doesn't contain any fighting, so yes, it's only for the students who are very enthusiastic in the field of medicine.

Theodore: Oh! This is archetype Jennae is in!

Jamie Lucus: Who's Jennae?

Theodore: She is the daughter of the doctor.

Jamie Lucus: The Doctor? Who's that?

Theodore: I don't know much about him, just that he really takes care of me and is good in medicine.

Draco Sapphire: Next comes the Angelic Archetype, the most powerful of all the archetypes, only the best and strongest go into this one. So, let's talk about its perks, students admitted into this archetype receive training of magic, categorized into two points. When reaching the first point, also known as the Sevagoth, it will allow the user to gain 155% more power to his base strength. When a user reaches the second and most powerful point of the Angelic Archetype, the user receives the ability to fly, the ability to go invisible, the ability gives and restore other user's mana and above all else the user gains some resistance to dark mana attacks.

Jamie Lucus: This is what I am joining Theodore and you should too, we would easily be at the top of the classes.

Theodore: I like this one but let's here out the last one.

Jamie Lucus: It's the Insignia archetype, it's the worst one out of the lot, why would you want information on that one.

Theodore: Its good know everything before taking the first step.

Jamie Lucus: Come on man, you are so boring!

Draco Sapphire: Finally, the last one is the Insignia Archetype. Its one of the lesser chosen archetypes but is a unique and powerful archetype, nevertheless. Students admitted into this archetype receive training of magic and this archetype is categorized into four points. It is basically used by high level mana users who generally lack full control over their power. The four points are named as

- Insignia Release
- Insignia Shadow
- Insignia Judgement
- Insignia Requiem

Insignia release helps its user to a much finer form, peaceful mindset, and better critical thinking capabilities. Insignia shadow allows its user to replicate his mana into a shadow clone, which he can use to teleport and cover vast distances. Insignia judgement, is a little dangerous but it relaxes the body and encourages more mana outflow, increasing the deadliness of the mana attack and increases the radius of the attack. Finally, we come to Insignia Requiem, it can only be used, and I mean only, when the situation is dire enough that it makes the user feel that if mana isn't enough, he can use his life force and increasing the deadliness of the attack but in return it takes away the time you have left to live. Don't worry you will hardly ever use it and in this Modrose, its application is forbidden. Finally, every student shall now be given a form and he can freely select any archetype of their choice.

Theodore: I think I made up my mind, I am going to choose the Insignia Archetype!

Jamie Lucus: Do what you want! Remember this, the archetype you are choosing is the worst.

Theodore goes to the form table and selects the Insignia Archetype. Sir Draco Sapphire see him and goes up to him and tells him that it is the right choice for him and that he needs to work very hard to control his overwhelming power. After two hours, Sir Draco Sapphire tells the students that the induction ceremony has concluded, and they can go to their assigned rooms. But Sir Draco Sapphire tells Theodore to stay back for a while because he needs to talk about very important things regarding his future in the Modrose, School Of Witchcraft. After the auditorium is empty, Sir Draco Sapphire confronts Theodore.

Draco Sapphire: Theodore, what are you hoping to achieve in this school?

Theodore: I want to understand and learn how to control my powers, that's it sir.

Draco Sapphire: A wise decision, do you know what you are?

Theodore: What I am? I am just an ordinary boy, sir.

Draco Sapphire: No! child you are a God Seed! The highest rank, a mana user can acquire in this school.

Theodore: Really? Am I that good?

Draco Sapphire: Good is a subjective term here, I haven't seen anyone more powerful than you, at your current age.

Theodore: Is that bad?

Draco Sapphire: Only time will tell child! Just so we are clear, if you go rogue, remember this you will be shown no remorse.

Theodore: Understood sir!

Theodore then turns his back on Sir Draco Sapphire and leaves the auditorium. Sir Jackson Felix, the headmaster appears in the room and confronts Sir Draco Sapphire.

Jackson Felix: So, do you think this boy is trouble?

Draco Sapphire: When did you come here?

Jackson Felix: I was here since the start; the boy is a kindhearted young man, but his abilities are terrifying to say the least.

Draco Sapphire: Yes, sir but we can never let our guard down.

Jackson Felix: Keep a close eye on him Draco, if he ever turns rouge, tell me as quickly as possible.

Draco Sapphire: Don't worry sir, I will report to you whenever he does so.

Sir Jackson Felix vanishes, and Sir Draco Sapphire starts to think about the uncertain future and prays to God for a good future for the world and for the future of the establishment.

6 The Plan

Eager to attack, Satan called forth a conference in hell to settle the fate of Adamazious once and for all. All the powerful generals and the seven princes of hell were called upon by Satan. On receiving the call to the palace, all the generals and the seven princes rushed to the palace to settle this matter once and for all.

Satan: It has been far too long, and I say it is the perfect time to strike. The Korodians have been destroyed and now we have a clear path to Adamazious.

Zonia: Sire! Please appoint me to kill this pitiful waste of life!

Satan: Hush! even you know you can't rival what he is right now!

Zonia: My apologizes, Sire!

Mammon: Sire! Send Beelzebub and I to fight this creature. We will return with its head!

Beelzebub: Yes, Sire! He wouldn't be able to take on two of us at once!

Satan: So be it! Bring his lifeless body to me and I shall grant you whatever you so desire!

Mammon: Consider it done, Sire!

Satan: Take this filth with you too, you need all the help you can get!

Zonia: Sire! I thank you! You will not be disappointed.

The inhabitants of hell all rejoice and cheer for Mammon, Beelzebub and Zonia. All the inhabitants gather around them and start to feed them their demonic essence, this makes them even more powerful, as the demons feed on any negative emotion or aura around them. With their strength and speed amplified, they prepare for their upcoming battle with Adamazious.

7

The Arrival Of Evil

It has been three years since being enrolled in Modrose and Theodore has now become very knowledgeable in mana usage and in the arts of the Insignia Archetype. The school has announced a preparatory leave to its students for twenty days. Every student starts to pack up their things and plan their trips to go back home and meet their loved ones. Theodore gets a message from Jennae that he must meet up on the bus station near the school and the message also said that the doctor will be there to pick them both up. Theodore excitedly starts to change into a relaxing attire and packs his things in his bag and heads out towards the bus station. He spots Jennae there and is amazed how fast she has grown. This was because the boy's and girl's dorm room were separate, and the classrooms were also separate, so they couldn't see each other during classes and nor during school hours. They both were amazed to see each other all grown up and they both patiently waited for the doctor to arrive. After an hour, the doctor arrives and meets both. He is happy to see Theodore all grown up and with a smile, he hugs him tightly and asks them both to get in the car. Along the way, the doctor has a conversation with them both.

Doctor: How was your time in Modrose, Theodore?

Theodore: It was very fascinating to say the least, I met very interesting people and I learned a lot about controlling my powers too!

Doctor: Oh, that's marvelous! What about you Jennae?

Jennae: It was freaking hectic, the new courses are very hard, but you know me, I still aced them!

Doctor: That's my daughter for you! She a chip off the old block, I tell you! Also, I have something exciting planned before we reach home!

Jennae: Oh really! Where are you going to take us?

Doctor: Don't want to ruin the surprise!

Theodore: Well, you got me excited now!

After three hours have passed, the doctor tells them both that they are nearing their destination, and both should get ready. They arrive at an old farmhouse and the doctors tells both of them to step outside the car and check the old farmhouse out. Before stepping outside the car, Theodore feels something odd about the farmhouse but doesn't utter a word.

Doctor: To all of you, this may look like just another old farmhouse, but this is the place where I got married.

Jennae: Oh My God! Dad why didn't you take me here sooner?

Doctor: I was going too but due to the death of your mother, I just didn't have it in me.

Theodore: I am sorry to hear that doctor.

Doctor: Theodore my name is Aister Moore, stop calling me "The Doctor", I am not a superhero.

Theodore: Well, I never got the chance to ask you for your name.

Aister Moore: Well now you know child.

Jennae Moore: HAHAHAHAHHAHA.

Theodore, Aister and Jennae all make their way inside the farmhouse and start to look around. Theodore walks outside and leaves both in and starts to look around. Suddenly the sky turns blacker and blacker, Theodore senses demonic presence around the area and rushes into the house.

Theodore: Both of you stay in the house and don't come out, we are all in danger right now!

Aister Moore: What do you mean danger?

Jennae Moore: Dad! Look outside, its three o'clock and the sky is pitch black. Theodore does it mean what I think it does?

Theodore: Yes! I can sense demonic presence here!

Jennae Moore: But that's impossible, the higher ups of our school have set a protective barrier to keep them out of earth.

Theodore: That must be for the weaker ones! The ones I sense are far more powerful to hold back!

Jennae Moore: What do we do?

Theodore: Stay inside, I am going to fight them.

Jennae Moore: Are you crazy! Going alone will get you killed or severely injured!

Theodore: We don't have a choice right now, keep your dad close to you and run away when I give you the signal!

Theodore: And Jennae if I don't make it, just run, and don't look back!

Jennae Moore: WHAT ARE YOU SAYING? ARE YOU CRAZY? WE AREN'T GOING TO LET YOU FIGHT THEM ALONE!!!!

Theodore: Calm down, a single death is better then many more. I promise you I will survive this!

Jennae Moore: Good luck Theo!

Theodore leaves both in the house and steps out of the house and into the fields. The demonic presence is becoming more and more prominent and this really unsettles Theodore. Red lightening strikes the ground revealing Mammon, Beelzebub and Zonia.

Mammon: Greeting Adamazious! I am Mammon, I am the first prince of hell. This is my brother Beelzebub, the third prince of hell and beside him is Zonia, the most powerful general of hell!

Theodore: Adamazious? My name is Theodore Truesdale!

Mammon: No, your useless ball of festering flesh, that is the name given to you by God!

Theodore: Wait! What do you mean?

Beelzebub: So, the most powerful creation of God doesn't even know his real name! HAHAHAHA, what a sad sight!

Mammon: And here I was concerned about our fates. His power level is that of mere human, I really feel sorry for you, INSECT!

Theodore: Shut it! I can control my power; I have purposely lowered my power!

Mammon: You are a funny one! Do you really think an insect like you stands a chance against our demonic might?

Beelzebub: Let's not waste our time and let's kill this nuisance!

Zonia: I agree, the faster the better! We are going to enjoy tearing you, limb from limb, BOY!

Theodore: Bring it!

Mammon commands Zonia to attack first, he charges into Theodore, who castes a barrier but Zonia's fist breaks though it and Zonia successfully hits Theodore on the chest, which sends Theodore flying towards a large tree. The tree breaks down but luckily Theodore, in time, castes a barrier around his back which protect him from a serious injury. Zonia follows the strike with a demonic slash attack, which Theodore narrowly avoids. The princes start to laugh at this pathetic show of power.

Mammon: Are you still holding back, insect?

Beelzebub: You are so weak that a pion like Zonia is winning against you. Zonia finish him!!!

Zonia: Yes! my lord, this attack will seal his fate!

Zonia charges up for his final attack and Theodore stands up and signals Jennae to leave! Both Jennae and Aister Moore start running away from the farmhouse. The princes don't realize the signal and laugh away.

Zonia: Die WORM! ENIGMA BURST!!!!!

The attack connects and the area around them crumbles and there is fire everywhere.

Zonia: AHAHHAHAHAHHAHA, the insect is dead!!!

Mammon: What a letdown this creature was!

Beelzebub: AHAHAHAHAHAHAHAHA

Theodore: You done laughing, BIG MOUTH?!!!

Zonia: THIS IS IMPOSSIBLE! HOW DID YOU SURVIVE THAT, WITH THAT KIND OF POWER LEVEL?

Theodore: Do you really think someone as weak as you, has a chance against me?

Zonia: DON'T MOCK ME WORM!

Theodore: INSIGNIA RELEASE!!!!!

Zonia: WAIT, YOUR POWER LEVEL.... ITS...ITS... ITS INCREASING? HOW ARE YOU DOING THIS??

Theodore: You had your chance, now it's my turn, prepare yourself!

Zonia: You don't scare me! GIVE ME YOUR BEST SHOT WORM!!!!!!!!!

Theodore: SOLAR FLAME!!!!!!

Zonia: AAAAAAAAAAAAAAAAAAAAAA ..........NOOOOOOOOOOOO!!!!!!!!........... HOW IS THIS POSSIBLE..... DAMN YOUUUUUUUUUUUUUUUUU!!!!!!!!!!!!!!!!!!!!!

Mammon: FINALLY! You weren't lying about suppressing your power!!! But let me warn you insect, WE ARE WAY POWERFUL COMPAIRED TO THAT FILTH!!!!!!

Both Mammon and Beelzebub, start to release their auras, the area around them goes blackish purple. The pressure their auras create is very unsettling to Theodore, but he stands his ground and starts to release his aura. The ground beneath them starts to crack open and furious winds start blowing around them. Theodore charges up first and castes another Solar Flame at both, but they stand their unfazed and still powering up. Theodore is a little shocked because that attack didn't even faze them.

Mammon: Do you really think that puny attack will work against us, INSECT?

Beelzebub: WE ARE GOING TO POUND YOU UNTIL THERE IS NOTHING LEFT OF YOU.

Theodore: SHUT UP AND FIGHT ME!!!!!

Both Mammon and Beelzebub strike Theodore down and start pummeling him. Both unleash a savage barrage of punches and kicks. At this point, Theodore is in so much pain that he thinks he is going to die. Mammon and Beelzebub then pick him up and threw him across the farmhouse and into the lake. Then they fly up to the sky and charge for one last blow.

Mammon: This will mark your end, INSECT!!!

Beelzebub: GET READY TO MEET YOUR MAKER!

Suddenly, Mammon gets blasted by seven streams of light and falls to the ground. Beelzebub looks around and finds Modrose's Headmaster and senior teachers behind him. Beelzebub looks at the Jackson Felix with disgust.

Beelzebub: So, you all want to die?

Jackson Felix: Shut it! foul demon, I'll never let you touch any of my students! Draco hurry up and treat Theodore!

Draco Sapphire: On it, Sir!

Mammon: You bunch of insects; I will grind your bones to dust!

Jackson Felix: Gandalf, Alexander III, Storm Bringer, Hellspawn and Colt Sapphire, lets take these menaces out!

All of them charge into one another and all hell breaks loose.

Sir Draco Sapphire dives into the lake and gets Theodore out. He immediately castes a healing spell on him and his body starts to heal up quickly. After a few minutes, Theodore quickly gets up and looks here and there but is told to calm down by Sir Draco Sapphire.

Theodore: Sir! There are two demons left!

Draco Sapphire: WAIT WHAT? THERE WERE MORE?

Theodore: Yes, but I defeated the 3rd one but the rest of them are super powerful!

Draco Sapphire: WAIT! YOU ARE TELLING ME YOU DEFEATED A DEMON?

Theodore: Yes sir! But we don't have time left! They are after me so hurry up and leave me be sir!

Draco Sapphire: No need to be a hero, the headmaster and other senior teachers got this in the bag!

Theodore: No sir! You don't understand, if they are fighting them, they don't have much time left, we must help them right away!

Draco Sapphire: The headmaster is no joke, child. He can take both on single handedly!

Theodore: Sir, trust me on this one! They don't have a clue what they are up against!

Theodore: INSIGNIA SHADOW!!!!

Both Theodore and Draco Sapphire teleport to the fight and when they reach the area, they are horrified to see what had happened. They find all the heads of the senior teachers and headmaster impaled with dark spears. Sir Draco Sapphire falls to the ground and starts crying for the death of his father, Colt Sapphire! Theodore immediately hugs him and tells him that they need to keep moving and find those demons. Draco Sapphire get furious and yells at Theodore to leave him alone. Theodore understands his emotions and uses Insignia Shadow to teleport near the place where the sky is pitch black and the area around is blackish purple. He finds them both there, search for him.

Theodore: HEY, YOU TWO, LOOKING FOR SOMEONE!

Mammon: HUH! So, the insects finally show up! You should have stayed lost!

Beelzebub: Were those old hags your reinforcement? The oldest hag some power but in the end, it was pointless, WORMS ARE WORMS AFTERALL! AHHAHAHAHAHHAHAHAH!

Theodore: HEY! STOP SAYING THAT!!!!!

Mammon: Oh, don't cry, insect. You will soon join them! AHAHHAHAHAHAHAH!

Theodore: Come at me with everything you got, I AM DONE HOLDING BACK!

Mammon: Done holding back? You little insect, last time we went easy on you but this time, we will put an end to your pitiful existence!

Beelzebub: No Mammon! let me deal with this pest!

Mammon: The stage is your brother!

Beelzebub charges at Theodore with full force, clinching his fit, impowered with demonic essence. This time Theodore readies himself early and this time he wants to strike back with brute force. Just as soon as Beelzebub's attack misses, Theodore does something risky.

Theodore: INSIGNIA JUDGEMENT!!!!!

Beelzebub: YOU LITTLE INSECT, HOW DARE YOU EVADE MY ATTACK!

Theodore: ICE BLAZE!!

Theodore's attack hits and seriously injures Beelzebub.

Beelzebub: HOW DARE YOU STIKE ME WITH YOUR FLITHY MAGIC!!!!!!

Theodore: I TOLD YOU I AM NOT HOLDING BACK ANYMORE, THIS FIGHT IS OVER, TWIN GAMMA BURST!!!!

Beelzebub: DAMN YOU PESKY HUMAN!! YOU GOT ME!!!!!

Beelzebub falls to the ground in pain. Mammon runs to his aid and throws a fire ball to create distance between Beelzebub and Theodore. Mammon picks Beelzebub up and then stares at Theodore.

Mammon: You know brother what must be done, right?

Beelzebub: Yes! it must be done to please our lord!

Mammon: I witness thy sacrifice and promise thi that it shall not go in vain!

Mammon stabs Beelzebub in the chest and takes out his heart. He then devours his heart and suddenly Mammon's aura starts to increase. Theodore feels that something is wrong, the pressure created from Mammon's aura, is unsettling to him. Theodore takes a stance and readies himself again, Mammon sees him and starts to laugh hysterically.

Mammon: HAHAHAHHAAHAHA, INSIGNIFICANT WORM!!!! DO YOU REALLY THINK YOU CAN DEFEAT ME NOW?

Theodore: I HAVE TOO, IT'S THE ONLY WAY TO SAVE THE LIFE ON THIS PLANET!!!!!

Before Theodore can make a move, Mammon hits him with his COLLACIUM BARRIAGE. Every punch and every kick get heavier and more powerful, one after another. At this point, Theodore can only block the attacks targeted on his vital organs but due to the immense speed of Mammon, Theodore receives many lethal blows, causing him to fall to the ground.

Mammon: You fought well, INSECT. But you know what they say, A GOOD INSECT IS A DEAD INSECT!!!!!!!!!!!! DIE!!!!!!!!!!!!!!!!!

Just when Mammon is about to put Theodore out of his misery, he gets interrupted by a huge mana blast from the sky. Mammon investigates the sky and finds Sir Draco Sapphire.

Draco Sapphire: YOU WILL NOT GET AWAY WITH THIS, YOU INSIGNIFICANT F PIECE OF FILTH!!!!!!!!!!

Mammon: Such a bore, you are! HUMAN!

Sir Draco and Mammon charge at one another and a huge collision takes place. After the rubble and dust settles, Theodore sees Mammon's hand impaling through Sir Draco's chest.

Theodore: oh no! OH NO!!!!!!!!!!!!!!!!!!!!!!!!

Mammon: Pitiful human, did you really think you had the physical strength or speed to match a high-ranking demon?

Draco Sapphire: You piece of filth; I am not going to hell WITHOUT YOU!!!

At that precise moment, Draco knows that this would be his final stand against the demon. Even knowing that he has broken through the first two points of the war archetype, he still thinks he's got a chance.

Draco Sapphire: WAR: DARK CORNOR!

Theodore: NO!!! Sir Draco DON'T PUSH YOURSELF!!!!!!!!

Mammon: OHHHHH!!! THIS IS SURELY INTRIGUING!!

Draco Sapphire: THEODORE! FIND THE STRENGTH TO RUN AWAY FROM THIS PLACE. I WILL HOLD HIM OFF, RUN MY CHILD RUN!!!!!!!!!!!!!!!!!!!!!!!!!!!!

Mammon: OH, WHAT A SAD SIGHT, DO YOU REAILY THINK YOU CAN BECOME A LONG ENOUGH DIVERSION, WITH A WOUND LIKE THAT?

Draco Sapphire: I KNOW THAT DAMN IT! BUT IF SAVING A LIFE MEANS I FOR GO MINE, IT'S A CHOICE I AM WILLING TO TAKE! NOW GET READY DEMON!

Mammon: AHHAHAHHAHAHHAAHAHHAHAHAHH! I WILL MAKE THIS END QUICKLY, LITTLE WORM!!!

They both exchange heavy blows with one another, and their fighting is so intense that it causes the ground to crack open with every blow. Theodore runs away as per Sir Draco's request but soon after covering a good distance, using Insignia Shadow, he looks back and there is dust and rubble everywhere from where those two are fighting. The impacts and shock waves created from their fists meeting one another, could be heard, and felt miles away. This goes on for three hours and suddenly, there is one huge sound and one last huge shock wave that is felt by Theodore. Theodore feels at unease because he knows that one of them has struck a killing blow. Fearing the worst, Theodore uses Insignia Shadow to see what happened. As the dust clears away, Theodore sees that Mammon has lost a whole arm while the whole lower torso of Sir Draco Sapphire is missing. Theodore uses Insignia Judgement to blast Mammon to a distance and then uses Insignia Shadow to get Sir Draco away from Mammon. Mammon after being blasted away, lays low and starts to heal himself. After covering a good distance, Theodore sees that Sir Draco Sapphire was starting to lose consciousness and slowing succumbing to his injuries.

Theodore: Sir, please don't leave me, I can't defeat this foe all by myself!!!

Draco Sapphire: Dear child, why do you always underestimate yourself? You have the power to undo him, you only need to dig deeper and find the you who can eradicate him! You may not know it but I for know that you can do it! You have the strength! I KNOW BECAUSE I FELT IT IN OUR ENCOUNTER, YOU CAN DO THIS, DON'T LET ME AND THE OTHERS DOWN!

Theodore: HOW DO I DO IT? TELL ME SIR, HOW DO I REACH SUCH A LEVEL?

Draco Sapphire: That I leave up to you to find out! And Theodore protect the life I cherished! Give it everything you got to protect it! If it comes down to giving away your own life? Just remember there is NOTHING NOBLER THAN SELF-SACRIFICE!

Just as Sir Draco Sapphire says these words, a tear role down his eyes and he lets off a simple smile.

Theodore: S..SI.....SIR!!PLEASE DON'T LEAVE ME SIR!!!!!!!

While Theodore is screaming, it just so happens that Jennae and Aister Moore see him and immediately rush towards him.

Jennae Moore: THEO, WHAT HAPPENED WHY ARE YOU CRI.......SI....SIR... DRACO??? WHAT HAPPENED TO HIM?

Theodore: PLEASE CAN YOU HEAL HIM?

Jennae Moore: With the state he is in, there is nothing anyone can do! I AM SORRY THEO! HE IS LONG GONE!

Theodore: IF ONLY I WAS STRONG ENOUGH! IF ONLY I COULD GET STRONGER!

Suddenly, everything goes still, its as if everything froze but Theodore is still able to move and look around. He looks around and then looks towards the sky and find something with wings coming down to the surface.

Gabriel: Greetings Adamazious! It is I, Gabriel!

Theodore: My name is Theodore! not Adamazious and isn't that the name of one of God's most trusted angels?

Gabriel: Yes, you have heard correctly about me. Your real name is Adamazious, you are made of God's own blood. Theodore Truesdale is your human name! You were made to annihilate Satan, the seven princes and all the inhabitants of hell!

Theodore: Wait, I am made up of God's blood? And how am I supposed to defeat Satan, the seven princes and the inhabitants of hell, if I can't even beat this demon right here?

Gabriel: AHHAHAHAH, you can totally beat this weakling, you just need to believe in yourself! You are made up of God's own blood, your strength is beyond even you, try to let go your earthly ways and try to be carefree for once and not think about anything nor anyone!

Theodore: I am afraid if I let loose, I believe I can cause harm to everyone here.

Gabriel: Sometimes, one must make sacrifices for the greater good! Keep that in mind next time you face Mammon again!

Theodore: I understand now, maybe it's the only way!

Gabriel: Good luck to you Adamazious, God has high hopes for you!

Adamazious: Trust me, I will not disappoint my creator!

The meeting ends and Gabriel flies up in the sky and suddenly vanishes. Everything starts to become normal and Theodore gets up and digs a grave for Sir Draco Sapphire. After making the grave, he covers Sir Draco with his long shirt and then lowers him down. After lowering him down, he fills the grave back up and then looks in the sky.

Theodore: I died for a noble cause, please undo his sins and grand him a better resting ground. I beg thi!

Aister Moore: Who are you talking to Theodore?

Theodore: Just a prayer!

Aister Moore: I see, he meant a lot to you, right?

Theodore: He was a great individual.

Theodore senses danger again and tells both Aister and Jennae to get far away from this place as possible. Both Aister and Jennae start running away but out of nowhere Mammon lands in front of them and tosses them aside with fury, they fall to the ground unconscious. Seeing this, Theodore blasts him with his ICE BLAZE, Mammon blocks the attack but due to the power behind the attack he gets pushed back a long way. Theodore furiously runs towards Mammon and prepares himself for the final confrontation.

Theodore: Surrender! Its for your own good, you can't beat me now!

Mammon: Do you think you can beat a prince? Don't be delusional you PEST, I WILL POUND YOU TO OBLIVION!!!

Theodore: FOR SOMEONE AS WEAK AS YOU, YOU SURE TALK A LOT!

Mammon: DON'T MOCK ME, INSECT!!!!!!!!!!!!!

Mammon charges at Theodore with full might, clenching his fist and mumbling evil spells to enhance his strength. Before Mammon strikes, Theodore uses a binding spell, which traps Mammon in his tracks.

Theodore: AHAHHAHAHAHAH, I am so disappointed in myself, how was I getting beat by someone like you?

Mammon: YOU INSIGNIFICANT INSECT, YOU THINK YOU CAN HOLD ME?

Theodore: Holding you, no I am merely just charging my attack to undo you from existence! And there is nothing you can do about it!

Mammon: HAVE MERCY!! ILL TURN OVER A NEW LEAF!!! I WON'T HURT ANYONE FROM NOW ON, PLEASE LET ME LIVE!!

Theodore: Your crimes against mortals far outweighs your kindness, farewell foul DEMON! SOLAR JOLT!!!!!

The attack hits Mammon and a huge explosion takes place. The dust and rubble settle, and Theodore sees that Mammon has survived but he knows that Mammon is holding on to his last strings of life. So, he un-castes the binding spell because he thinks that the fight has been won.

Theodore: AHHAHAHHAH, I commend you on surviving that! But your abilities have been severely crippled, you can't fight me now!

Mammon: Damn you!

Theodore charges again for another Solar jolt, Mammon looks around for something to defend himself and finds Aister Moore. Knowing that he is going to die if he doesn't do anything, he makes a desperate attempt to possess Aister Moore. Mammon turns into smoke and moves quickly towards Aister, Theodore sees this and castes a binding spell again, but he is too late. Mammon possess Aister and he knows that Theodore can't kill an innocent creature. With command over Aister's body, Mammon charges at Theodore and strikes him with many brutal blows, which causes Theodore to fall to the ground.

Aister (Mammon Controlled): How does it feel?

Theodore: You won't get away with this!

Aister (Mammon Controlled): HAHAHHAHAHAH but as you can see, I ALREADY HAVE!!! THE ONLY WAY YOU CAN TAKE ME OUT IS IF YOU DESTROY HIM, HAHAHAHAHH!!!!

Theodore: LEAVE HIM ALONE! WHAT HAS HE EVER DONE TO YOU?

Aister (Mammon Controlled): Do you really think I can let go of this opportunity to end you? HAHAHAHHAHAH.

Just as Mammon speaks these words out of Aister's mouth, suddenly Aister starts talking to Theodore.

Aister Moore: THEO MY BOY! I DON'T WANT TO YOU AND THE REST OF THE WOLRD TO SUFFER, PLEASE RELEASE ME OF THIS DEMON.

Theodore: I CAN'T REMOVE HIM FROM YOU, I WOULD HAVE TO KILL YOU!!

Aister Moore: If that is what it takes to finish this vile creature, so be it. CLENSE ME OF MY SUFFERING!!!!

Aister (Mammon Controlled): Do you really think he is going to kill you; HE IS TOO KINDHEARTED TO DO SUCH A THING. AHHHHAHAHHAHAHAH!

Theodore: I HEAR YOU LOUD AND CLEAR AISTER, MAY GOD HAVE MERCY ON YOU AND GIVE YOU NUMERIOUS BLESSINGS FOR YOUR SACRIFICE!

Theodore begins to charge his solar jolt again and Mammon sees this and charges towards him. Mammon unleashes numerous blows on Theodore, but Theodore doesn't respond and keeps on charging. From a distance, Jennae finally gains consciousness and sees what is happening, she sees her father striking Theodore while Theodore is charging for an attack. She starts rushing towards to break up the fight but as soon as she reaches halfway, she witnesses Theodore unleash his Solar Jolt on his father, instantly obliterating him. She falls to the ground screaming and Theodore sees her and rushes towards her.

Theodore: I am sorry, Jennae. It was the only way to end this.

Jennae Moore: YOU MONSTER, YOU KILLED MY FATHER!!!!!!!

Theodore: You got it all wrong, he was possessed by Mammon! There was nothing I could do save him except by killing him along with Mammon.

Jennae Moore: YOU MURDERER, THESE ARE ALL LIES, I DON'T BELIEVE YOU!

Theodore: I am not lying; you have got to believe me!

Jennae runs off and yells at Theodore to never come in her sights ever again. Theodore tries to stop her but fails.

8

The New Order

The news of Mammon, Beelzebub and Zonia reaches hell and Satan is outraged by this. He orders another conference to be held and invites the rest of the princes and generals of hell. All the princes and high-ranking generals of hell come to the conference room in Satan's Castle.

Leviathan: DON'T KNOW HOW? DON'T KNOW WHY, BOTH MAMMON AND BEELEZBUB GOT DEAD BY WORM!!!!

Satan: HUSH!!!! Leviathan!!!!!!!!!!!!!!

Leviathan: NGH!!!!!!!! SORRY!!!!!!

Satan: Two princes of hell and the most powerful general, we had been killed by that creature! What do we do now?

Azazel: WAR! WAR IS THE ANSWER!

Satan: You make a valid point Azazel, a war with Adamazious? A full-on frontal assault? I like it.

Azazel: TOO MANY AT ONCE, HARD TO COUNTER. WILL MAKE IT EASY FOR US TO KILL PEST!

Satan: You do make a interesting case but I want something more sinister!

Belphegor: I heard the boy killed the father when he killed Mammon, why don't we bring the whore into this plan as well?

Satan: Trick the girl and lead Adamazious into a trap! After that, we rage WAR!!!

Belphegor: As you command, SIRE!

Satan: Send out the order of war but don't let the information about the girl to anyone!

Asmodeus: Your wish, is my command, my Lord!

The order reaches all in hell and the inhabitants of hell and the five princes of hell start to prepare for the war against Adamazious and Earth. A spy hears this and sends a message to Gabriel, this message was to warn Adamazious of the impending doom that has yet to come on Earth. Gabriel hears this and rushes to Adamazious.

9

The Training Begins

It has a year since the last demonic attack and things have calmed down a bit in Modrose. With the killings of the famous spellcasters, mana users and the headmaster, the school has become rather quiet. But a new staff has been appointed and Modrose is slowly but surely recovering. As of right now, there are final exams being held, so it is a busy time for the students of Modrose. Theodore for one is very confused, after knowing about what he is and what his main objective in life is. He is also worried about Jennae because he thinks that he could have had saved her father from that demon. He thinks to himself that he must fix his relationship with Jennae again, but he can't figure a way to do so. Suddenly, time stops, and everything freezes, Theodore is familiar with this and knows its Gabriel.

Gabriel: Greeting Adamazious! I hope, I am not disturbing you.

Adamazious: No, you are not, why are you here?

Gabriel: I am afraid, I have bad news!

Adamazious: Oh! How bad is it?

Gabriel: The situation has become dire, Satan along with the five remaining princes of hell, has assembled a huge army and is preparing for a final war with Earth, in hopes of taking you down for good!

Adamazious: WHAT?

Gabriel: You have heard me load and clear, you must prepare yourself and the inhabitants of Earth!

Adamazious: How much time do we have?

Gabriel: I don't exactly know but I think you have like two to three months before Satan and his forces launch their assault on Earth!

Adamazious: Do you think we can defeat them?

Gabriel: You are the Pinnacle of all creations; I leave it up to you to figure it out! Good day Adamazious, I pray the best for you and for this world!

Adamazious: WAIT! I NEED MORE INFORMATION!

Everything becomes normal again and now Theodore is under even more pressure than before. He thinks the best way to combat this threat is to talk to the new staff of the school. He rushes to the staff council room but is stopped by the guards there.

Theodore: Its urgent, sir!

Guard: We can't let you through, but we will notify the headmaster of your presence!

Theodore: We don't have time; I must speak to him right now!

Guard: It is prohibited for students to go in the staff council room!

Theodore: SIR, COME ON LET ME IN, THIS IS A VERY IMPORTANT MATTER!

Suddenly, the gates of the council room open and the headmaster walks out and confronts both the guards and Theodore.

Luke Gardner: What is the meaning of all this ruckus!

Guard: Sir, this boy has very important information!

Luke Gardner: Aren't you Theodore Truesdale?

Theodore: Yes sir, I seriously have very horrific news!

Luke Gardner: It's a pleasure to meet you Theodore! I am the new headmaster for Modrose, and my name is Luke Gardner. I have heard great things about you from the management! Come inside right away and tell me about the news!

Theodore and Luke Gardner both enter the room and Theodore is greeted by the rest of the staff members. Luke Gardner then tells the staff members that Theodore has some important news to tell us.

Theodore: Its really bad news, I have gotten word that Satan and his demons are planning to go to war with Earth.

Luke Gardner: Who told you this news? And how much time do we have to prepare ourselves?

Theodore: The holy angel Gabriel has told me about their plans, and we have roughly two to three months before they launch a full-scale war against us!

Luke Gardner: Pardon me, you mean Gabriel told you? The right-hand angel of God told you.

Theodore: You have heard me correctly, sir!

Luke Gardner: Don't mind this but what you are saying is hard to believe!

Theodore: Trust me, you may not know this, but my real name isn't Theodore as well, its Adamazious!

Kenchi Bayashi: You might be strong, but I think you are speaking lies. How can we believe you? Do you have any proof of this?

Stanis Oliver: I second this, maybe you are just delusional, this committee demands proof and without proof, you are just wasting our time.

Sarah Bilford: Theodore, both members are right, what proof do you have of this?

Carmen Alexander: Sorry boy, you need proof to your point across!

Suddenly, everything freezes but this time all the people in the room can move and see what is happening. The staff members all turn towards Theodore and find Gabriel behind him. All of them get star struck and in their amazement, they don't utter a single word.

Theodore: Everyone, the entity before you is Gabriel!

Gabriel: Greetings humans and Theodore! My name is Gabriel!

Luke Gardner: All glory to the mighty one!

Stanis Oliver: All glory to the mighty one!

Sarah Bilford: All glory to the mighty one!

Kenchi Bayashi: All glory to the mighty one!

Carmen Alexander: All glory to the mighty one!

Gabriel: Indeed! All glory is for my one and true lord! I am sure that all of you have gotten word from Adamazious that the great war is upon you?

Luke Gardner: Yes! we just got informed!

Gabriel: Great to hear, my part is done here, prepare well!

Luke Gardner: Wait, oh humble servant of God, could the angels help us in this cause?

Gabriel: We are to act only when God has given us the permission to do so. Good luck!

Everything becomes normal after the departure of Gabriel. Everyone is still in shock, but Adamazious gets up and tries to convince everyone.

Adamazious: Everyone we need to act fast; we don't have enough time left!

Luke Gardner: Do you have any ideas?

Adamazious: Well, I was thinking that the best choice we have against the demons is the Angelic Archetype, right?

Luke Gardner: Yes, their abilities provide a very good counter to demonic entities but could withstand their fury?

Adamazious: They have too, we only have one option. The WAR archetype can help too but its much riskier for them as well.

Kenchi Bayashi: Using Dark Corner might be the way to go for them, we will try to keep as many Light-sworn users as possible, so that when ever there is an injury, the Light-sworn users can help heal the wounded!

Adamazious: That's the perfect approach. The headmaster and I shall lead from the front lines.

Sarah Bilford: You are our main triumph card in this fight, wont it be a blunder to use you from the get-go?

Adamazious: You do make a valid point, but I am the strongest here, we need all the help we can get, storing me won't really help you.

Luke Gardner: Yes, he makes a valid point, order everyone in the school to start preparing for the war. All the restrictions on spells usage are lifted and tell the teachers that they can now teach the students powerful and forbidden spells too. We need all the help we can get now!

After saying that the council is disbanded and the news about the war spreads like wildfire through out Modrose. The final exams are called off and everyone, from student to teacher, is being trained for combat.

10

A Sinister Trap

After the order was given, the whole school was in complete war training. A new system of extenders was used in the Archetypes which would in turn increase the power of an individual when one reaches a certain point. The teachers named it the "Advance Network" and due to this network the Angelic, War and Insignia Archetype had gotten very strong boosts. The teachers also tried to fit in points of the Angelic Archetype with the rest of the archetypes, this gave the users demonic resistance and gave them attacks that could really damage demonic entities. Also, a new point was added into the War Archetype, Artemis, which gave the user the ability to yield a magical bow, which could shoot out heavenly light arrows, which could really damage demonic entities. The preparations were on full-force and a lot of progress was made, the headmaster and the staff members were now somewhat hopeful that so miracle could take place. After all that training, the students would go into their rooms and rest for the day and then repeat all that they did on the next day. It was a very tiring schedule but was compulsory for everyone, for it was essential for the fate of the Earth and humanity.

Jennae Moore was really troubled when she saw Theodore kill his father in front of her. She wasn't really training all that much and would mostly skip training sessions because her mind was coping with what had happened in front of her. She began to really hate Theodore but some part of her was trying to prove to her that Theodore did what he had to do to save her father. She never knew that it was her father who was possessed, and Theodore only had one way to save him, which was to kill him. If he hadn't done so, her father would burn in hell for all of eternity. Her hate for Theodore grew and grew, she wouldn't talk to him and would most of the times ignore him and walk away as fast as she could. She felt bad in doing so but she couldn't let go what he had done to his father.

One day when Jennae was lying in bed, thinking about Theodore, she felt something was odd but couldn't point her finger at it. Suddenly, Azazel appeared in front of her and began talking to her.

Azazel: Little girl, may I ask what are you thinking about?

Jennae: WHO ARE YOU AND HOW DID YOU GET INTO MY ROOM?

Azazel: There is no need to start yelling, I am but a friend! And I know everything that took place that day!

Jennae: You are a friend? What day?

Azazel: Yes, I am just a friend. The day when Theodore killed your father!

Jennae: You know about that day? What happened? I know Theodore can't kill an innocent person but why did he kill my father?

Azazel: Such a pity, you haven't seen the real face of Theodore.

Jennae: What do you mean?

Azazel: Theodore is a very powerful being, he only wants to rule the world with an iron fist. When your father got to know about his plans, he tried to stop him, but Theodore killed him, he did this because he wanted no one to interfere in his plans!

Jennae: To think that my father treated him with so much care and comfort, only to be back stabbed and killed by this ruthless brute. What do we do to stop him?

Azazel: I have a plan but it will be tricky, you have to promise me that you wont ever telling anyone of our meetings?

Jennae: Wouldn't more people help in this case? The more people we have, the more problems he will face.

Azazel: No, that will lead to more and more killing! Don't you understand we need to do this privately, as the great war is almost upon us, we need all the help we can get in that war, so doing this secretly is the way to go.

Jennae: I understand, what's your plan?

Azazel: A planned assassination!

Jennae: No!

Azazel: Don't you want to avenge your father?

Jennae: And level myself with that murderer? Never in a million years!

Azazel: We could always injure him severely and then lock him in? What do you say to that?

Jennae: Yes, that is a much better option!

Azazel: So be it, meet me in the auditorium tomorrow after the training sessions are over. We are going to contain him there!

Jennae: I understand but how are we going to lure him there?

Azazel: You are going to ask him to meet you there!

Jennae: No, I will not do that. HE MUDERED MY FATHER AND YOU EXPECT ME TO LURE HIM IN BY ASKING HIM TO MEET ME IN THE AUDITOIURM?

Azazel: No need to yell at me, how about writing a letter? It will be much easier, and you don't need to add in your name, so it will be anonymous!

Jennae: Great idea! We will do that!

Suddenly, Azazel disappears and leaves Jennae alone in her room to think about how she is going to lure him to the auditorium. The next day comes and Theodore finds a note places in his locker. He opens the note and starts reading it. The note reads:

"Dear Theodore Truesdale, please meet me in auditorium after the training session is over. I have something to talk to you about. From your secret admirer."

Theodore thinks about who could have sent him this and what could the person want to talk about. After the training session, he heads towards the auditorium.

Jennae and Azazel scheme on what do to next and they conclude that Jennae will distract Theodore and Azazel will follow her up and deliver a fatal blow to take down Theodore but not kill him.

Theodore reaches the auditorium and heads on in. He finds Jennae alone, sitting in a chair and reading a book. Theodore is happy that its Jennae and he hopes to talk to her and make her understand what really had happened between him and her father.

Theodore: Jennae, were you the one who wrote that letter?

Jennae Moore: Yes Theodore, it was indeed I who wrote that letter!

Theodore: I am so happy that it was you, I wanted to talk to you but never got the opportunity to speak to you!

Jennae Moore: Well, you killed my father, YOU MURDERER!

Theodore: I didn't murder your father; he was possessed by Mammon!

Jennae Moore: Lies, why did you just use your magic to expel him out of his body?

Theodore: It doesn't work like that, once a demon gets a hold of your body, only death can liberate you from the demon. If one isn't killed, he/she will spend his entire existence in hell, burning and serving Satan!

Jennae Moore: LIES! LIES! ALL OF THESE ARE LIES! YOU KILLED SOMEONE WHO LOVED YOU! TREATED YOU LIKE IF YOU WERE HIS OWN! WHY! WHY!

Theodore: I didn't kill him because I wanted to. I killed him to release him from his suffering.

Jennae Moore: LIES! MY FRIEND TOLD ME THAT YOU ONLY WANT WORLD DOMINATION! AND WHEN MY FATHER FOUND OUT ABOUT YOUR PLANS! YOU KILLED HIM IN COLD BLOOD!

Theodore: YES! I AM EVIL! WASN'T I THE ONE WHO WAS RISKING HIS OWN LIFE WHEN FIGHTING THOSE THREE DEMONS? WASN'T I THE ONE WHO TOLD YOU GUYS TO RUN AND NEVER LOOK BACK? WHY WOULD I EVER KILL THE PEOPLE I LOVE SO MUCH? THOSE PEOPLE FOR WHOM I WOULD GIVE UP EVEN MY OWN LIFE!

Jennae Moore: I DON'T UNDERSTAND! YOU ARE SAYING THIS AND MY FRIEND WAS SAYING THAT WHO CAN I TRUST?

Theodore: Your friend? There was no one there when I was fighting your father! Everything around us was in flames! Did you see anyone around you?

Just as Jennae was going to answer, Azazel appears behind Theodore and stabs him with a huge sword. The sword through the left side of his back and comes out of his chest. Jennae see this and is in total disbelief. Azazel then starts to laugh and grin at Jennae.

Jennae: You promised you wouldn't kill him!

Azazel: YOU LITTLE SLUT! DID YOU REALLY THINK I WAS A GOOD GUY? THIS WAS MY PLAN ALL ALONG AND THANKS TO YOU I CAN KILL THIS PEST! HAHAHAHAHAHHA.

Jennae: YOU TRICKED ME! I WON'T LET YOU DO THIS!

Azazel: Tricked you? NO, I TOLD YOU EVERYTHING AND YOU AGREED TO EVERYTHING! I HAVE NO PART IN THIS, YOU BEGGED ME TO TAKE REVENGE FOR YOUR FATHER! AND TO TOP IT ALL OFF, HE WAS TELLING YOU THE TRUTH ABOUT YOUR FATHER! THE INSECT GOT POSSESSED AND THE ONLY WAY TO SAVE HIM WAS TO KILL HIM! AHHAHAHAHAHHAHA.

Jennae: YOU CAN'T DO THIS!

Azazel picks up his sword again and heads towards Theodore to kill him. Jennae stops him in his tracks and stands in front of Theodore, with her arms open.

Jennae: I WON'T LET YOU HURT HIM!

Azazel: GET OUT OF MY WAY, YOU WHORE!

Azazel slashes at Jennae's stomach and tosses her aside. He jumps in the air but gets caught in a binding spell, casted by Sir Luke Gardner and Sir Kenchi Bayashi. Both order the rest of the staff members to take the students out of the auditorium and use containment spells to seal the auditorium. The auditorium gets sealed and both Jennae and Theodore are escorted out of the auditorium. Sir Luke Gardner and Kenchi Bayashi uncast the binding spell and ready themselves for a confrontation against the demon.

Luke Gardner: You foul Demon! How dare you come here?

Azazel: Releasing me from that binding spell is the last mistake you will ever make! And I will make sure of that!

Kenchi Bayashi: Get ready you demon scum! We are going to obliterate you!

Azazel: You? YOU PESKY HUMANS ARE GOING TO HURT ME? DON'T MAKE ME LAUGH!

Luke Gardner: SAY WHAT YOU WANT DEMON, YOU WILL KNOW THE TRUE MIGHT OF MORTALS!

Azazel: HAHAHHAHAHAH, BRING IT ON PESTS!

Luke Gardner: WAR Archetype, ADVANCE: ARTEMIS RESOLVE.

Azazel: What kind of sorcery is this? I can't move and I can't use my powers! DAMN YOU PESTS!

Kenchi Bayashi: We got help from Gabriel! Let see what this heavenly bow can do! ARTEMIS DIVINE ARROW!!!!

Azazel gets hit with the arrow and is in so much pain that he starts to melt.

Azazel: WHAT IS THIS? HEAVENLY LIGHT? SPARE ME AND I WILL TELL SATAN TO KEEP YOU TWO ALIVE AND HE WILL BESTOW UPON YOU WITH RICHES!

Luke Gardner: Do you think we are dumb enough to listen to a fucking DEMON? ARTEMIS DIVINE ARROW!

Azazel: DAMN YOU PESTS! IT DOESN'T MATTER YOU SEE, FOR MY LORD HAS AN ADVANTAGE NOW! ADAMAZIOUS IS FATALY WOUNDED, THERE IS NO CHANCE YOU CAN WIN THIS WAR NOW, SO LONG PESTS!

Azazel dies and both the headmaster and Sir Kenchi Bayashi rush to check on both Jennae and Theodore. They reach the nursing room and they both get notified that Jennae is getting better and will recover in a day or two, but Theodore may not make it. This really frustrates the headmaster because he knows how important Theodore is in this war, so he asks the medical staff to give it everything they got.

11

True Evil Descends

The news about Adamazious, being fatally injured, reaches hell. Satan calls forth a meeting and asks every prince and general to come as soon as possible. All of them arrive at the palace and enter the council room.

Satan: Adamazious has been fatally wounded! We should attack Earth right away!

Belphegor: AHAHAHAHAH, WAR WAR WAR!!!!!!!!!!!!!!!!!!!!!!!!!!!!

Leviathan: Sire! Give the order and we shall slay every pest there is on Earth!

Satan: Losing Azazel is a big loss, but we have weakened our adversary! We shall bring about total darkness to the whole universe. READY THE ARMIES AND DIRECT THEM TOWARDS EARTH!

Asmodeus: HAIL SATAN!

Belphegor: HAIL SATAN!

Leviathan: HAIL SATAN!

Lucifer: HAIL SATAN!

Satan and his fleet march towards Earth, they use portals, which links hell to Earth.

Back on Earth! Gabriel is seen talking to Sir Luke Gardner and the rest of the staff.

Gabriel: Satan army is upon you! Gather the strength you have and meet him in combat and fight like there is no tomorrow!

Luke Gardner: Do you think we have a chance against Satan without Adamazious?

Gabriel: No! it will be a miracle if you do but as it stands you will only be prolonging the inevitable!

Kenchi Bayashi: What if Adamazious dies?

Gabriel: I think you know the answer to that question, don't you?

Luke Gardner: Sir Bayashi, order the school to gather around and get ready for the final confrontation of their lives!

Gabriel: You are a fine man! Sir Luke! I salute you!

Gabriel disappears and an army fifty thousand soldiers, comprising of teachers and students marches outside the school doors and waits for the arrival of Satan's forces. Suddenly, portals start to appear in front of them and they see demonic soldiers coming out, fully armed and in numbers that would terrify any living being.

The headmaster joins the first lane and asks everyone to stand their ground and adjust themselves to the formations they were told. With a huge force of a hundred million strong and armed soldiers, Satan enters Earth and orders his army to attack. The demonic soldiers charge will full force, the headmaster orders the WAR archetype users to join the front lines and activate the ARTEMIS point, they shoot out arrows of light, which in turn decimate the front lines of Satan forces but this doesn't really make a dent on his forces, as there are so many, it hardly makes a difference. The air assault continues, the headmaster then orders the WAR and Angelic Archetype to join the front lines and attack on foot. The headmaster leads the way and there is an all-out brawl, the students and their headmaster were fight valiantly but then Satan orders Lucifer and Leviathan to join the demonic soldiers. Lucifer and Leviathan charge at the fleet and completely decimates it, the headmaster gets decapitated and the students are eaten alive by both the demon soldiers and the princes. The school's army is forced to retreat and lock themselves behind school doors with five hundred spellcasters casting a barrier to not let the enemies get through. Sir Kenchi runs to check on Theodore and finds out that he is in very critical condition and his final hour is upon him. Kenchi and Stanis both run into the nursing room and the try to wake Theodore up.

Kenchi Bayashi: WAKE UP THEODORE, YOUR SCHOOL NEEDS YOU!!! YOUR PEOPLE NEED YOU!

Stanis Oliver: YES, WAKE UP THEODORE, WE NEED YOU!

Jennae Moore, Malissa Armstrong and Jamie Lucus enter the room and each of them start to say a little chant.

ALL MIGHTY REJUVINATOR OF THE HEAVENS AND SKY
I BEG TO THI PLEASE HEAR MY CRY
IF EVIL DWELLS WITHIN THIS PLACE
PLEASE MAKE IT LEAVE THIS SPACE
TRANSFORM THIS MORTAL FROM ORB OF HEAVENLY LIGHT
AND BRING US VICTORY IN THIS GREAT FIGHT
I BEG THI, WHOS MIGHT ENVELOPS ALL
MAKE THE GOOD STAND TALL
AND SEAL THE FATE OF EVIL WITH A HEFTY FALL

Suddenly a flash of light hits Theodore and everyone gets blown away. After the dust and rubble settles, everyone sees Theodore completely healed and walking outside the school's nursing room. Both Kenchi Bayashi and Stanis Oliver catch up to him and tell him what had happened.

Kenchi Bayashi: Adamazious, we have lost our headmaster, please lead us now!

Adamazious: Sir! Open the gates and let your army charge at full force and don't interfere with the princes and Satan, those guys are my responsibility now!

Stanis Oliver: Understood, may God be with you!

The barrier gets broken and the door is broken, and the army of Satan starts to pour in. To their surprise, Adamazious is standing in front of them and he yells at the top of his voice, "CHARGE". Satan's army gets pushed back and with Adamazious, the battlefield is now leveled. Adamazious goes full on ballistic and unleashes his solar jolts, these solar jolts kill nearly half of the Satan's forces. Satan, now being scared, orders the rest of the princes to attack Adamazious. The princes and demonic soldiers all charge at Adamazious and all hell breaks loose. Millions of demonic soldiers are destroyed while a handful of students lose their lives, mostly since Adamazious was both fighting and protecting them. Both Kenchi and Stanis join the fight and are ordered by Adamazious to attack the rest of the fleet and leave the princes of hell to him. Adamazious and the princes meet and all of them charge at one another but this time Adamazious isn't holding back and tosses them back with powerful spells. The teachers and students fight valiantly, and the once huge demonic army is completely decimated and destroyed. Finally, Satan stands up and joins the fight, Satan kills all the princes of hell and absorbs their demonic essence. Then he orders his fleet to give up all their demonic essence and make him stronger. The fleet does so, and Satan grows and power, then he looks towards Adamazious and charges towards him. He lands a hit on Adamazious, which sends him flying into the schools building. Adamazious get seriously injured and falls to the ground, inside the school. Satan starts to laugh and grin at the remaining humans.

Satan: Did you ever think you were going to defeat me? PESTS? I HAVE DEFEATED YOUR HERO, NOW THERE IS NOTHING YOU CAN DO TO STOP ME, BETTER YET I WILL END THIS RIGHT NOW!

Satan flies into the sky and charges up a huge black energy ball, it keeps getting bigger and bigger and finally Satan throws it down towards land. The teachers and students all stand up and charge up their mana and all of them direct their mana beams towards the energy ball to push it back. Satan smile and yells at the humans.

Satan: Do you think your pip squeak attacks can push back my negative eclipse energy ball? I don't think so, It may surprise you that I have only used forty percent of my power up till now! YOU DON'T HAVE ANY CHANCE OF WINNING THIS BATTLE! SAY GOODBYE TO YOUR EARTH! YOU PESTS!

12

The Last Stand

Jennae runs towards the school and looks for Theodore's body. She finds it near the gate, surrounded with rubble and then talks to him.

Jennae: ADAMAZIOUS WE NEED YOU! PLEASE COME BACK TO US! YOU ARE THE ONLY ONE THAT CAN SAVE US FROM COMPLETE ANNHILATION! I KNOW I AM A BAD PERSON TO HAVE TRICKED YOU BUT NOW I KNOW WHAT A KIND SOUL YOU REALLY ARE! I DON'T WANT YOU TO DIE! PLEASE COME BACK TO ME THEO!

Suddenly, Theodore starts to wake up and tells Jennae that everything is going to be fine and he is going to do everything in his power to beat Satan once and for all. They both share a passionate kiss and Theodore rushes to the battlefield. He finds everyone in a beam struggle and see the enormous black energy ball coming down on Earth.

Adamazious readies himself and charges his final attack. After charging he releases his IGNITION BEAM, all their beams combine into one and with the help of Adamazious the huge black energy ball gets pushed back slowly. Satan now fearing the worst, puts everything he has into his final attack. The pressure becomes so great that some of the students and teachers die as a result. After one hour it looks as if they even with their combined strengths, they can't defeat Satan. Satan laughs at them and continues to push the energy ball down. Adamazious knowing that if this energy ball hits the ground, it will destroy everything. Adamazious has a final look around and then tears roll down his eyes.

Adamazious: Sir Kenchi and Stanis, retreat right away!

Kenchi Bayashi: What do you mean?

Stanis Oliver: You aren't thinking what I think you are, right?

Adamazious: Sir! It's the only way, please understand and retreat!

Kenchi Bayashi: We need you Adamazious, you don't have to do this!

Adamazious: The life of many is more important than the life of one individual! Please understand and retreat, right now!

Kenchi Bayashi: Goodbye Adamazious, may God have mercy on you!

Kenchi Bayashi orders everyone student and teacher to retreat into the school and hide until all of this is over. Jennae hears this and starts to cry and runs into the battlefield, Sir Stanis stops her and tell her that Adamazious has given the command to retreat but she still hesitates and tries to run again but this time Sir Stanis knocks her unconscious by gently tapping her on the neck, by which she falls to the ground and is then picked up and retrieved to the school.

Adamazious has a good look and sees that there is no one remaining on the battlefield. He smiles and then starts to communicate with Satan himself.

Adamazious: So, it has come to this!

Satan: YOU INSECT, I AM DESTROY EVERYTHING YOU HOLD DEAR!

Adamazious: I WON'T LET YOU!

Adamazious suddenly uses the last and most dangerous point of the Insignia Archetype, Insignia Requiem, his beam becomes more powerful and now it's a standstill between both. Satan laughs at Theodore and says that its still not enough. Adamazious reveals that he is yet to play his triumph card and suddenly, he activates Insignia Requiem,

Advance: Ultimate Requiem. This causes his beam to become even more powerful and is powerful enough to push back Satan's Negative Eclipse Ball back at him, killing Satan as a result.

Everyone comes out of hiding and start rushing towards the battlefield, they find Adamazious on the ground. They pick him up and bring him back to the school, the teachers there start asking him questions, but he doesn't respond to any of them. Sir Kenchi Bayashi bends a knee and is seen crying, Jamie Lucus walks towards him and asks him why he is crying.

Jamie Lucus: Sir! Why are you crying on a moment like this one, you should be celebrating! Adamazious has won us the war and by the looks of things, he is so tired that he can't even utter a word.

Kenchi Bayashi: Don't you see child? The great hero has died, Adamazious is no more with us!

Jamie Lucus: But he only used Requiem for a little while, he can't be dead!

Kenchi Bayashi: That wasn't the simple Insignia Requiem, it was Ultimate Requiem, it takes away his life forces, 100 times faster then the usual Requiem. He gave up his own life to protect ours!

Jamie Lucus can't handle his emotions and starts crying so hard that everyone hears him and rushes to him. He explains them what had truly happened and there was dead silence in the school and after that everyone start to cry. When Jennae heard about this news, she immediately rushed towards the body of Adamazious and hugged it. She cried her heart out and after sometimes she suddenly stopped, everyone checked on her and found out that she had passed away herself.

The next day both Adamazious and Jennae were buried in the school's graveyard and every person was invited and to their burial ceremony and the day was set to be a memorial day in the history of Modrose.

9 798885 551045

Printed by Libri Plureos GmbH in Hamburg,
Germany